Copyright © 2002 by Nord-Süd Verlag AG, Gossau Zürich, Switzerland
First published in Switzerland under the title *Der Biber geht fort*
English translation © 2002 by North-South Books Inc., New York

First published in the United States, Great Britain, Canada,
Australia, and New Zealand in 2002 by North-South Books,
an imprint of Nord-Süd Verlag AG, Gossau Zürich, Switzerland.

Distributed in the United States by North-South Books Inc., New York.

Library of Congress Cataloging-in-Publication Data is available.
A CIP catalogue record for this book is available from The British Library.
ISBN 0-7358-1564-X (trade edition) 10 9 8 7 6 HC 5 4 3 2 1
ISBN 0-7358-1565-8 (library edition) 10 9 8 7 6 LE 5 4 3 2 1

For more information about our books, and the authors and artists
who create them, visit our web site: www.northsouth.com

Printed in Belgium

Old
Beaver

By Udo Weigelt

Illustrated by Bernadette Watts

Translated by
Sibylle Kazeroid

North-South Books
New York/London

The beaver had lived along the river at the edge of the forest for many years. One day he realized that he was getting old. Each log he carried felt heavier and heavier. It took him longer and longer to fell a small tree. To tell the truth, Old Beaver was tired. He didn't feel like building dams anymore.

Old Beaver began to spend his days sunning himself on the roof of his lodge.

Soon the other animals noticed that Old Beaver did nothing but relax.

"This is not good," declared Owl. "A proper forest with a proper river needs a beaver who builds proper dams!"

The animals decided to look for a new beaver—one who was young and strong.

Old Beaver soon heard about their plans. Well, he thought sadly, I suppose that the animals are right. I'm just a nuisance here. The forest needs a new beaver, and since there's no room for two beavers, I'd better just go away.

So Old Beaver set out, even though leaving wasn't easy and he didn't really know where to go.

Soon Old Beaver grew tired. He crawled into a tree hole and fell fast asleep.

That same day, the animals brought a new beaver to the forest. He was young and very strong.

Young Beaver set to work right away. But his first dam collapsed, even though he had worked very hard on it. He just didn't know how to build a proper dam yet.

"What did I do wrong?" he cried impatiently.

The other animals couldn't tell him. They didn't know any more about building dams than Young Beaver did.

Then Young Beaver had an idea. "What happened to your old beaver?" he asked.

"I think he is in his lodge," said Badger.

Young Beaver shook his head. "The lodge is empty."

For the first time, the animals realized that Old Beaver had disappeared. Suddenly they found that they missed him, whether he built dams or not.

So they all ran off to look for him. They
looked everywhere—especially along the river.

The birds flew about looking for Old Beaver, and the forest echoed with the sound of all the animals calling his name. They were so noisy that . . .

. . . they woke up Old Beaver.

"Why are you making such a racket?" he cried. "I'm old, but I'm not deaf!"

"Here you are!" said Hedgehog happily. Then he called to the other animals, who quickly gathered around.

"Why did you leave?" asked Owl reproachfully. "You can't just disappear without telling anybody!"

"Well, I thought if you got a new, young beaver you wouldn't need me anymore," said Old Beaver.

"That's not true," said Rabbit. "The forest needs older animals. Who else can we ask for help when we don't know something?"

"Exactly!" said Young Beaver. "I desperately need your help with my dams."

"You must come back, Old Beaver!" cried the animals.

But Old Beaver wasn't listening. He and Young Beaver were heading down to the river, deep in a discussion of dam building.

The other animals stood watching them.

"Don't worry," Old Beaver called over his shoulder.

"I'm staying, after all. There is still some work for me

to do."

Old Beaver went back to sunning himself on the roof of his lodge. From there he could see the river and call out advice to Young Beaver on building proper dams.

He didn't build any dams himself, but that didn't bother the other animals. They were just happy to have him back.